MR. BOUNCER'S HOUSE

TRUNDLEBE...

FIRE STATION

BLODGER'S GATEHOUSE

SIGMUND SWAMP'S HOUSE & BOATHOUSE

FERNYBANK FERRY

BROCK GRUFFY'S SHOP

BRAMBLE'S FARM

CHURCH

VICARAGE

RAILWAY STATION

P.C. HOPPIT'S HOUSE

POLICE STATION

DR. BUSHY'S HOUSE

N
W E
S

This book belongs to:

....

PUBLISHED BY PETER HADDOCK LIMITED, BRIDLINGTON, ENGLAND.
© FERN HOLLOW PRODUCTIONS LIMITED.

GRANNY BOUNCER'S RESCUE

Written and Illustrated by John Patience

The day for the annual seaside trip had arrived and Fern Hollow railway station was packed with excited animals; buying tickets, showing off new buckets and spades and exclaiming to each other what a perfectly beautiful day it was. As was usual for this occasion, a special train had been booked and, as it drew into the station puffing out steam and smoke, an enormous cheer went up from the children.

Eventually everyone had got themselves settled in the train and were impatient to be off, but there was a problem. Granny Bouncer had not yet arrived. "Perhaps she isn't well," some animals suggested. "Maybe she has forgotten about the trip," others said. At last, just as the train was about to leave without her, Granny came running down the platform. "I forgot my knitting," she panted, waving a multicoloured object on the end of her needles. "I had to go back for it."

The guard blew his whistle and Mr Rusty the engine driver
started the train. Soon they were rushing through the open
countryside. The children looked out of the windows, there
was a lot to see; a scarecrow, a windmill and a canal with
lots of little boats on it. Meanwhile Granny Bouncer

concentrated on her knitting, occasionally pausing to pop a
humbug into her mouth. Suddenly the train puffed round the
side of a hill and there was the sea, all sparkling and blue in
the morning sunshine!

At Brineybeach Station the animals bustled out of their carriages and sniffed the air. It was filled with the wonderful, exciting smell of the sea. Soon everyone was down on the beach. The children and some of the more daring older animals changed into their swimming costumes. Some went for a paddle or a swim in the sea. Others watched the Punch and Judy show.

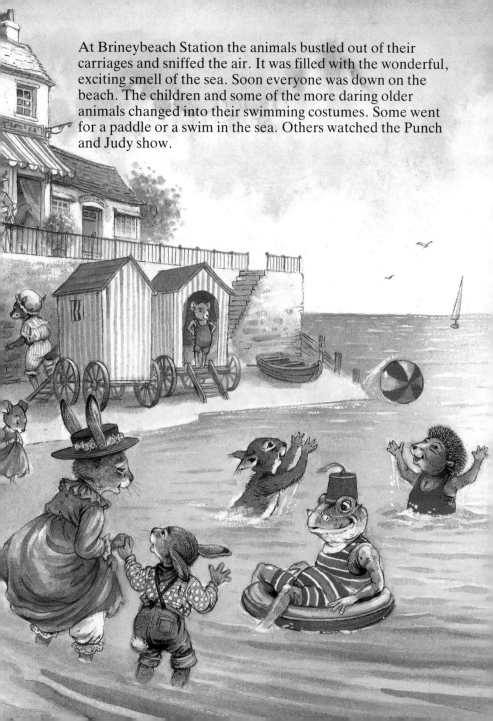

The children began to build sand castles and a competition was held to choose the best one. It was won by Jiggy and Jasper Acorn, whose castle was at least twice as big as the others and had lots of little flags stuck into it. Unfortunately, later in the afternoon the tide began to come in and washed the castle away. Then Jasper began to cry, but he was soon cheered up when Mr Acorn bought him an icecream cornet.

At last the sun began to slip down on the horizon and the air grew cooler. Then everyone changed out of their swimming costumes back into their warm clothes. It was decided at this point that they would all go for a walk along the pier. Granny Bouncer went along too, but she quickly found a deck chair and got on with her knitting. She had been busy all afternoon and had produced a very, very, very long scarf.

Pippa Bouncer climbed on to the pier railings and sat her
teddy bear on them so that it could look at the sea. Then
something terrible happened. The teddy bear slipped out of
Pippa's hands and, as she made a grab at it, she fell off the
pier and splashed down into the sea. There was a general
panic on the pier with no-one knowing what to do. Then
Granny Bouncer came to the rescue. She lowered one end of
her enormous scarf down to Pippa who, of course, clung on
to it like a limpet. "Heave-ho!" cried Granny, and everyone
hauled Pippa up to safety. The poor little rabbit was rather
wet and frightened but otherwise quite all right.

It had been a very eventful day, but now it was time to go home. The train journey back to Fern Hollow was not as exciting as the one they had made that morning, but everyone was feeling happy and contented. Most of the children fell asleep, while the adults chatted about the day's events. As for Granny Bouncer, all that could be heard from her was the clicking of her knitting needles!

Fern Hollow

MR. CHIPS'S HOUSE

MR. WILLOWBANK'S COBBLERS SHOP

MR. CROAKER'S WATERMILL

STRIPEY'S HOUSE

SCHOOL

THE JOLLY VOLE HOTEL

RIVER FERNY

MR. ACORN'S BAKERY

MR. RUSTY'S HOUSE

MR. PRICKLESS HOUSE

POST OFFICE

BORIS BLINK'S BOOKSHOP

MR. TWINKLE'S HOUSE

MR. TUTTLEEBEE'S SHOP

MR. THIMBLES TAILORS SHOP

WINDYWOOD